HORRiD HENRY
and the
Bogey Babysitter

HORRID HENRY
and the
Bogey Babysitter

Francesca Simon
Illustrated by Tony Ross

Orion
Children's Books

Horrid Henry and the Bogey Babysitter originally appeared
in the black and white storybook of the same title
first published by Orion Children's Books in 2002
This edition first published in Great Britain in 2013
by Orion Children's Books
a division of the Orion Publishing Group Ltd
Orion House
5 Upper Saint Martin's Lane
London WC2H 9EA
An Hachette UK Company
1 3 5 7 9 10 8 6 4 2

Text © Francesca Simon 2002, 2013
Illustrations © Tony Ross 2013

The Orion Publishing Group's policy is to use papers that
are natural, renewable and recyclable products and made
from wood grown in sustainable forests. The logging and
manufacturing processes are expected to conform to the
environmental regulations of the country of origin.

A catalogue record for this book is available from the British Library.

Printed in China

www.orionbooks.co.uk
www.horridhenry.co.uk

For the inspirational Arlene Phillips

There are many more **Horrid Henry** books available.
For a complete list visit
www.horridhenry.co.uk
or
www.orionbooks.co.uk

Contents

Chapter 1

"No way!" shrieked Tetchy Tess,
slamming down the phone.

"No way!" shrieked Crabby Chris,
slamming down the phone.

"No way!"
shrieked Angry
Anna. "What do
you think I am,
crazy?"

Even Mellow Martin
said he was busy.

Mum hung up the phone
and groaned.
It wasn't easy finding someone
to babysit more than once for
Horrid Henry.

When Tetchy Tess came,
Henry flooded the bathroom.

When Crabby Chris came he hid her homework and "accidentally" poured red grape juice down the front of her new white jeans.

And when Angry Anna came Henry – no, it's too dreadful. Suffice it to say that Anna ran screaming from the house and Henry's parents had to come home early.

Horrid Henry hated babysitters.
He wasn't a baby.
He didn't want to be sat on.
Why should he be nice to some
ugly, stuck-up, bossy teenager
who'd hog the TV and pig out
on Henry's biscuits?

Parents should just stay at home
where they belonged, thought
Horrid Henry.

And now it looked like they would
have to. Ha! His parents were mean
and horrible, but he'd had a lot of
practice managing them.

Babysitters were unpredictable.
Babysitters were hard work.
And by the time you'd broken them
in and shown them who was boss,
for some reason they didn't want
to come any more.

The only good babysitters let you stay up all night and eat sweets until you were sick. Sadly, Horrid Henry never got one of those.

Chapter 2

"We have to find a babysitter,"
wailed Mum.
"The party is tomorrow night.
I've tried everyone.
Who else is there?"

"There's got to be someone,"
said Dad. "Think!"

Mum thought.
Dad thought.

"What about
Rebecca?"
said Dad.

Horrid Henry's heart missed a beat.
He stopped drawing moustaches on
Perfect Peter's school pictures.
Maybe he'd heard wrong.
Oh please, not Rebecca!
Not – Rabid Rebecca!

"Who did you say?" asked Henry.
His voice quavered.

"You <u>heard</u> me," said Dad. "Rebecca."

"NO!" screamed Henry.
"She's horrible!"

"She's not horrible," said Dad.
"She's just – strict."
"There's no one else," said Mum
grimly. "I'll phone Rebecca."

"She's a monster!" wailed Henry.
"She made Ralph go to bed at
six o'clock!"

"I like going to bed at six o'clock," said Perfect Peter. "After all, growing children need their rest."

Horrid Henry growled and attacked. He was the Creature from the Black Lagoon, dragging the foolish mortal down to a watery grave.

"AAAEEEEE!" squealed Peter. "Henry pulled my hair."

"Stop being horrid, Henry!" said
Dad. "Mum's on the phone."

Henry prayed. Maybe she'd be busy.
Maybe she'd say no.
Maybe she'd be dead.

He'd heard all about Rebecca.
She'd made Tough Toby get in his
pyjamas at five o'clock *and* do all
his homework.

She'd unplugged Dizzy Dave's
computer.

She'd made Moody Margaret
wash the floor.

No doubt about it, Rabid Rebecca
was the toughest teen in town.

Henry lay on the rug and howled.
Mum shouted into the phone.

"You can! That's great, Rebecca. No, that's just the TV — sorry for the noise. See you tomorrow."

"NOOOOOOOO!"

wailed Henry.

Chapter 3

Ding dong.

"I'll get it!" said Perfect Peter.
He skipped to the door.

Henry flung himself on the carpet.

"I DON'T WANT TO HAVE A BABYSITTER!"

he wailed.

The door opened. In walked the biggest, meanest, ugliest, nastiest-looking girl Henry had ever seen.

Her arms were enormous.
Her head was enormous.
Her teeth were enormous.
She looked like she ate elephants for breakfast, crocodiles for lunch, and snacked on toddlers for tea.

"What have you got to eat?"
snarled Rabid Rebecca.

Dad took a step back.
"Help yourself to anything in
the fridge," said Dad.

"Don't worry, I will," said Rebecca.

"GO HOME, YOU WITCH!"
howled Henry.

"Bedtime is nine o'clock,"
shouted Dad, trying to be heard
above Henry's screams. He edged
his way carefully past Rebecca,
jumped over Henry, then dashed
out the front door.

"I DON'T WANT TO
HAVE A BABYSITTER!"

shrieked Henry.

"Be good, Henry," said Mum weakly.
She stepped over Henry,
then escaped from the house.

The door closed.
Horrid Henry was alone in the
house with Rabid Rebecca.
He glared at Rebecca.
Rebecca glared at him.

"I've heard all about you, you little
creep," growled Rebecca. "No one
bothers me when I'm babysitting."

Horrid Henry stopped screaming.
"Oh yeah," said Horrid Henry.
"We'll see about that."

Rabid Rebecca bared her fangs.
Henry recoiled.

Perhaps I'd better keep out of her way, he thought, then slipped into the sitting room and turned on the telly.

Chapter 4

Ahh, *Mutant Max*. Hurray!
How bad could life be when
a brilliant programme like *Mutant
Max* was on? He'd annoy Rebecca
as soon as it was over.

Rebecca stomped into the room and
snatched the clicker.

ZAP!

DA DOO, DA DOO DA, DA
DOO DA DOO DA, tangoed some
horrible spangly dancers.

"Hey," said Henry. "I'm watching
Mutant Max."

"Tough," said Rebecca.
"*I'm* watching ballroom dancing."

Snatch!

Horrid Henry grabbled the clicker.

 # ZAP!

"And it's mutants, mutants, mut—"

Snatch!

ZAP!

DA DOO, DA DOO DA, DA DOO
DA DOO DA.
DOO, DA DOO DA, DA DOO DA
DOO DA.

Horrid Henry tangoed round the
room, gliding and sliding.

"Stop it," muttered Rebecca.

Henry shimmied back and forth
in front of the telly, blocking her
view and singing along as loudly
as he could.

"DA DOO, DA DOO DA,"
warbled Henry.

"I'm warning you," hissed Rebecca.

Perfect Peter walked in.
He had already put on his blue
bunny pyjamas, brushed his teeth
and combed his hair. He held a game
of Chinese Chequers in his hand.

"Rebecca, will you play a game with
me before I go to bed?" asked Peter.

"NO!" roared Rebecca. "I'm trying
to watch TV. Shut up and go away."

Perfect Peter leapt back.
"But I thought — since I was all ready
for bed…" he stammered.

"I've got better things to do than
to play with you," snarled Rebecca.
"Now go to bed this minute,
both of you."

"But it's not my bedtime for hours,"
protested Henry. "I want to watch
Mutant Max."

"Nor mine," said Perfect Peter
timidly. "There's this nature
programme…"

"GO!" howled Rebecca.

"NO!" howled Henry.

"RAAAA!" roared Rabid Rebecca.

Chapter 5

Horrid Henry did not know how it happened. It was as if fiery dragon's breath had blasted him upstairs. Somehow, he was in his pyjamas, in bed, and it was only seven o'clock.

Rabid Rebecca switched off the light. "Don't even think of moving from that bed," she hissed. "If I see you, or hear you, or even smell you, you'll be sorry you were born. I'll stay downstairs, you stay upstairs, and that way no one will get hurt."

Then she marched out of the room and slammed the door.

Horrid Henry was so shocked he could not move. He, Horrid Henry, the bulldozer of babysitters, the terror of teachers, the bully of brothers, was in bed, lights out, at seven o'clock.

Seven o'clock!
Two whole hours before his bedtime!
This was an outrage! He could hear
Moody Margaret shrieking next door.

He could hear
Toddler Tom
zooming about
on his tricycle.

No one went to bed at seven o'clock.
Not even toddlers.

Worst of all, he was thirsty.
So what if she told me to stay in bed,
thought Horrid Henry. I'm thirsty.
I'm going to go downstairs and
get myself a glass of water. It's my
house and I'll do what I want.

Horrid Henry did not move.

I'm dying of thirst here, thought
Henry. Mum and Dad will come
home and I'll be a dried out old stick
insect, and boy will she be in trouble.

Horrid Henry still did not move.

Go on, feet, urged Henry, let's just
step on down and get a little ol'
glass of water. So what if that bogey
babysitter said he had to stay in bed.
What could she do to him?

She could chop off my head
and bounce it down the stairs,
thought Henry.

Eeek.

Well, let her try.

Horrid Henry remembered who he was. The boy who'd sent teachers shrieking from the classroom.

The boy who'd destroyed the Demon Dinner Lady. The boy who had run away from home and almost reached the Congo.

I will get up and get a drink of water,
he thought.

Chapter 6

Sneak. Sneak. Sneak.

Horrid Henry crept to the
bedroom door.
Slowly he opened it a crack.

Creak.

Then slowly, slowly, he opened the door a bit more and slipped out.

ARGHHHHH!

There was Rabid Rebecca sitting at the top of the stairs.

It's a trap, thought Henry.
She was lying in wait for me.
I'm dead, I'm finished, they'll find
my bones in the morning.

Horrid Henry dashed back inside
his room and awaited his doom.

Silence.

What was going on?
Why hadn't Rebecca torn him
apart limb from limb?
Horrid Henry opened his door
a fraction and peeped out.

Rabid Rebecca was still sitting
huddled at the top of the stairs.
She did not move. Her eyes were
fixed straight ahead.

"Spi–spi–spider," she whispered.
She pointed at a big, hairy spider in
front of her with a trembling hand.

"It's huge," said Henry. "Really hairy
and horrible and wriggly and—"

"STOP!" squealed Rebecca.
"Help me, Henry," she begged.

Horrid Henry was not the fearless
leader of a pirate gang for nothing.

"If I risk my life and get rid of the
spider, can I watch *Mutant Max*?"
said Henry.

"Yes," said Rebecca.

"And stay up 'til my parents
come home?"

"Yes," said Rebecca.

"And eat all the ice cream
in the fridge?"

"YES!" shrieked Rebecca.
"Just get rid of that... that..."

"Deal," said Horrid Henry.

He dashed to his room and
grabbed a jar.
Rabid Rebecca hid her eyes as
Horrid Henry scooped up the spider.
What a beauty!

"It's gone," said Henry.

Rebecca opened her beady red eyes.
"Right, back to bed, you little brat!"

"What?" said Henry.

"Bed. Now!" screeched Rebecca.

"But we agreed…" said Henry.

"Tough," said Rebecca.
"That was then."

"Traitor," said Henry.

He whipped out the spider jar
from behind his back and
unscrewed the lid.

"On guard!" he said.

"AAEEEE!" whimpered Rebecca.

Horrid Henry advanced menacingly towards her.

"NOOOOOOO!" wailed Rebecca, stepping back.

"Now get in that room and stay there," ordered Henry. "Or else."

Rabid Rebecca skedaddled into the
bathroom and locked the door.

"If I see you or hear you or even
smell you, you'll be sorry you were
born," said Henry.

"I already am," said Rabid Rebecca.

Chapter 7

Horrid Henry spent a lovely evening
in front of the telly.

He watched scary movies.
He ate ice cream and sweets and
biscuits and crisps until he could
stuff no more in.

Vroom vroom.

Oops. Parents home.
Horrid Henry dashed upstairs
and leapt into bed just as the
front door opened.

Mum and Dad looked around the sitting room, littered with sweet wrappers, biscuit crumbs and ice cream cartons.

"You did tell her to help herself," said Mum.

"Still," said Dad. "What a pig."

"Never mind," said Mum brightly, "at least she managed to get Henry to bed. That's a first."

Rabid Rebecca staggered
into the room.

"Did you get enough to eat?"
said Dad.

"No," said Rabid Rebecca.

"Oh," said Dad.

"Was everything all right?"
asked Mum.

Rebecca looked at her.
"Can I go now?" said Rebecca.

"Any chance you could babysit on Saturday?" asked Dad hopefully.

"What do you think I am, crazy?" shrieked Rebecca.

SLAM!

Upstairs, Horrid Henry groaned.
Just when he had a babysitter
beautifully trained, for some reason
they wouldn't come back.